Zapato Power
FREDDIE RAMOS
POWERS UP

JACQUELINE JULES   art by KEIRON WARD

WITHDRAWN

Albert Whitman & Company
Chicago, Illinois

Don't miss the other **Zapato Power** books!

Library of Congress Cataloging-in-Publication data
is on file with the publisher.
Text copyright © 2022 by Jacqueline Jules
Illustrations copyright © 2022 by Albert Whitman & Company
Illustrations by Keiron Ward
First published in the United States of America
in 2022 by Albert Whitman & Company
ISBN 978-0-8075-9574-9 (hardcover)
ISBN 978-0-8075-9575-6 (ebook)

Printed in the United States of America

10 9 8 7 6 5 4 3 2 1 LB 26 25 24 23 22 21

For more information about Albert Whitman & Company,
visit our website at www.albertwhitman.com.

For Anna Hebner—JJ

For Mum Audrey, Dad Keith, and
Brother Mike—KW

Contents

1. Puppy

It was Saturday morning, the first day of spring break. My next-door neighbors at 28G were packing their car. Their dog, Puppy, was barking.

RUFF! RUFF!

Puppy barked like a dog who thought people were coming to see him, not leaving him to go away

for a week.

"*¡Buen viaje!*" Mom waved as the
Santos family drove off. They are
good friends of ours.

While they were gone, my
Uncle Jorge would be coming
from New York and staying in
their apartment with his new wife,

Angela, and her daughter, Juanita.

With Uncle Jorge and his family at 28G, Puppy could sleep in his own bed and eat from his own bowl. But someone had to walk him every day. That someone was going to be me.

RUFF! RUFF!

"Freddie!" Mom pointed as she turned to go inside. "Puppy's taking off again."

My neighbor's dog loves to chase squirrels. He is fast. But not too fast for me.

I touched a button on my wristband and raced off.

ZOOM! ZOOM! Zapato!

I have Zapato Power. My superpowered purple sneakers let me run ninety miles an hour, hidden in a cloud of smoke.

ZOOM! ZOOM! Zapato!

In a snap, I cornered Puppy and picked up his leash.

"Okay, Puppy," I told him. "Let's take a walk before Uncle Jorge gets here."

RUFF! RUFF!

Starwood Park, where we live,

has lots of buildings, sidewalks, and trees. It also has lots of squirrels. Puppy pulls on his leash every time he sees one. Luckily, I am stronger.

RUFF! RUFF!

We were going nowhere in circles until we ran into my first-grade friend Amy.

"Do you need help, Freddie?" she asked.

"Maybe," I admitted. "Puppy wants to run too much."

Amy grinned. "Let him loose. Together, we can keep track of him."

She was right. Amy has Zapato Power shoes too. Two kids with super speed could handle one short dog with lots of energy.

We both touched our wristbands, which control our superpowered shoes.

ZIP! ZIP! ZAPATO!

ZOOM! ZOOM! ZAPATO!

Amy and I stayed close to Puppy as he chased squirrel after squirrel.

RUFF! RUFF!

Puppy had the time of his life before he plopped down, too tired to bark.

While Puppy rested, Amy and I talked.

"I just saw Mr. Vaslov," she said. "He's busy in his toolshed."

"Making a new invention?" I asked.

Amy shrugged. "He could be. I don't know."

Mr. Vaslov is the best inventor on the planet. He made my superpowered purple sneakers. He made Amy's shoes too. She wears the super shoes I outgrew. Now we work as a team to do hero jobs at Starwood Park.

"I'm excited," Amy said. "I'm going to visit my grandparents for the weekend."

"My uncle Jorge and his family are visiting," I told her.

"Have fun!" Amy waved and zoomed off.

ZIP! ZIP! ZAPATO!

I picked up Puppy's leash and headed over to Mr. Vaslov's toolshed. If he was making a new invention, I wanted to know about it. Mr. Vaslov has a meteorite now. He keeps it on the shelf in his toolshed. Mr. Vaslov believes a rock from outer space could have special properties that would help with his superpowered inventions. Who knows what he could make now!

KNOCK! KNOCK! Mr. Vaslov didn't open the door. What did that mean? Was he busy making a flying jetpack? The thought gave me butterflies. KNOCK! KNOCK!

No answer. Mr. Vaslov was probably away fixing something. It's Mr. Vaslov's job to take care of Starwood Park.

RUFF! RUFF!

Puppy was tired of waiting, so I took him home to 28G. Once he was settled with a doggy treat, I went outside to look for Mr. Vaslov.

Around the corner, outside the laundry room, I saw his red electric scooter. A good sign he was nearby.

"Freddie!" Mr. Vaslov said. "So glad you're here. I need you!"

He sure did. The laundry

room in Building G had water
everywhere. What a mess!

2. The Yellow Gloves

"What happened?" I asked.

"A pipe broke," Mr. Vaslov explained. "I called our plumber, Mr. Willis, but he can't come until Monday."

It was only Saturday. The best we could do was clean up the water in the meantime. Not easy. The dripping mop went into a huge yellow bucket on wheels. You had to press hard on a lever to squeeze the water out.

"That's it, Freddie," Mr. Vaslov said. "Use a little more muscle."

Mopping didn't make me feel like a hero. Heroes are supposed to be strong. To squeeze the lever on the bucket, I needed more strength.

Mr. Vaslov looked around at all the stuff we had to move to finish cleaning.

"I need my work gloves," he said. "Can you get them for me, Freddie?"

That question made me feel better. Mr. Vaslov had bad knees and couldn't go quickly across Starwood Park, even on his electric scooter. But I could.

ZOOM! ZOOM! ZAPATO!

With my super speed, I made it to Mr. Vaslov's toolshed in a blink.

There I found the brown work gloves he always used when he lifted heavy things. And something else. On the shelf, right beside Mr. Vaslov's meteorite, was a pair of small yellow gloves. I tried them on, and they stretched perfectly over my hands. They even had little rubber dots on them to make

it easy to grip things. Maybe gloves could help me too.

I took Mr. Vaslov's brown gloves and the yellow ones back to the laundry room.

ZOOM! ZOOM! ZAPATO!

"May I use these?" I showed Mr. Vaslov the yellow gloves.

"Sure," he said. "They could help you work."

And they did! With the yellow gloves, I felt stronger. I could help Mr. Vaslov move a table and huge plastic boxes. I could even press the lever down to squeeze out the mop.

"Good job, Freddie," Mr. Vaslov said.

Did Mr. Vaslov know the yellow gloves were special? Were they a new invention?

"I like these yellow gloves," I said. "May I keep them?"

Mr. Vaslov shrugged. "Why not? I found them on the grass."

So the yellow gloves weren't Mr. Vaslov's newest invention. Could there be another reason they made me stronger? They'd been on the shelf, sitting beside the meteorite.

Hmm. The meteorite was from outer space. Maybe it gave off magnetic waves. Maybe some of its outer space power flowed into the gloves. Mr. Vaslov would like that!

Before we could talk about it, Mrs. Tran came to the door with a basket of dirty clothes. She wasn't happy to hear that the laundry room was out of order and she had to use the washers in Building H.

"I have a bad back," Mrs. Tran complained. "I can't carry this big basket so far."

"I'll do it," I offered.

Mr. Vaslov had taught me the

scientific method. If I wanted to find out if the yellow gloves made me stronger, I had to test them.

They didn't disappoint. With my yellow gloves, it was no trouble taking Mrs. Tran's dirty clothes to the next building.

"Thank you, Freddie!" Mrs. Tran said. "You're my hero."

Hero. That is my favorite word. And now with extra strength, I might be able to do even more hero jobs.

ZOOM! ZOOM! ZAPATO!

I raced back to 29G. Mom and her boyfriend, David, had another job waiting for me. They had just come back from the store.

"Look at these groceries!" David pointed at the trunk. "Your mom thinks she will be cooking for an army!"

"I'll carry them!" I said, reaching in with my yellow gloves.

"Are you sure, Freddie?" David asked. "These bags are heavy."

"Not too heavy for me!" Walking slowly, I carried four plastic bags of groceries at a time from the car to the kitchen.

Mom clapped. "My little boy is growing up and getting strong!"

I grinned. My yellow gloves might change my life!

3. Uncle Jorge, Aunt Angela, and Cousin Juanita

"I'm sorry I have to work," David told my mom.

David's company had a big business meeting, and he was going to be busy until late Sunday afternoon.

"But I'll be here tomorrow night." David kissed my mom.

She kissed him back. When David first came into our lives, he just took my mom out sometimes. No kissing in front of me. It was something I had to get used to.

"I can't wait for you to meet Jorge," Mom said.

"I hope your big brother likes me." David's eyes looked worried behind his black glasses.

"He will," Mom promised.

David left the house, and Mom got busy with dinner.

"Help me figure this out, Freddie," Mom said. "If it takes twenty minutes per pound, how

long should I cook a seven-pound
chicken?"

Mom made chickens in the oven
all my life and never wondered
how long to cook them before. We
both knew she was trying to make
me do math to keep up my grades.

But since I didn't have anything else to do until Uncle Jorge arrived, I multiplied.

"It takes 140 minutes to roast a seven-pound chicken."

From there, Mom gave me a division problem. "How many hours are in 140 minutes?"

Before Mom could trick me into any more math, we heard the sound of a car door closing.

Mom ran outside. "Jorge! It's been too long!"

My uncle hugged Mom tightly. "We need to get together more often."

"Not just at weddings." Aunt Angela smiled.

I hadn't seen my new aunt Angela since the day she married Uncle Jorge. That was a while ago, around the time Mom met David.

Everyone had been really dressed up at the wedding, including my new cousin, Juanita. She'd worn a long pink dress with her hair in a bun. She'd looked almost grown-up.

Now, at Starwood Park, Juanita was wearing jeans, and her hair was in a long braid. She seemed younger, more like someone I could be friends with.

"*Hola.*" Juanita waved at me.

When we finished saying hello, I got another chance to use my yellow gloves. Uncle Jorge was surprised I could lift the suitcases out of the trunk.

"Freddie!" Uncle Jorge said. "Those are heavy! When did you get so strong?"

"Or tall," Aunt Angela added.

The source of my new strength was my little secret. To test it again, I pulled the handles of two suitcases and dragged them behind me to 28G.

Puppy was excited to see people

when we opened the door. RUFF!
RUFF!

Uncle Jorge let Puppy sniff his
hand. Aunt Angela patted his
back. Juanita stood far away.

RUFF! RUFF!

"No te preocupes," I said. "Puppy won't hurt you."

"He'll jump on me." Juanita pressed her back against the wall.

"If you don't like Puppy," Mom offered, "you can stay with us at 29G. Our couch is comfy."

Juanita barely waited to hear her mom say it was okay. She grabbed her suitcase and dashed out the door.

Inside my bedroom, my new cousin met an animal she liked a lot better. My guinea pig, Claude the Second, is too small to jump on

people. As soon as he saw me, he stood up in his cage to beg for food.
WHEET! WHEET!

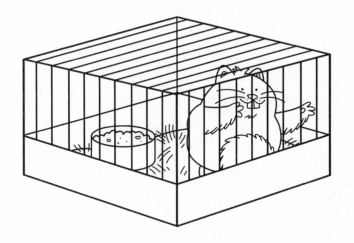

"*¡Qué lindo!*" Juanita said. "Can I feed him?"

I was glad Juanita thought Claude the Second was cute. That gave us something in common.

We also both liked Mom's chicken dinner. As everyone sat around the table eating, Uncle Jorge had some questions. First he asked if he could sleep in Sunday morning.

"I don't have vacation too often," he said.

"We'll all sleep in," Mom said. "This will be my vacation too."

The next question was more serious.

"When will I get to meet David, your boyfriend?" he asked.

"Sunday night dinner," Mom answered. "You're going to love him."

Uncle Jorge leaned back, folding his arms. "Don't get ahead of yourself, little sister. Let me decide what I think."

The look on Uncle Jorge's face worried me a little. How would Mom feel if her brother didn't like David?

4. The Pet Patch

In the morning, while Juanita and I ate cereal, Mom looked through her spice cabinet.

"*¡Ay, no!*" she cried. "*Necesito algo más.*"

"What do you need?" Juanita asked. "I'll go get it for you."

"Cinnamon," Mom answered.

"For my *arroz con leche*."

Juanita stood up. "Tell me where the nearest shopping center is."

"I can show you!" I jumped up from my chair.

Mom considered for a moment. "Freddie's not quite old enough to cross that busy street on his own. Together you should be okay."

Mom gave Juanita money, and we left the house wearing hats and coats. Soon I put on my yellow gloves too. It was a cold March day, so I had a good excuse. And I liked being ready if I needed extra strength.

At the crosswalk Juanita and I waited for the light to stop the traffic. When the sign said it was safe, we walked across the street together, like two big kids going shopping. Mom had said I was not quite old enough to cross the busy street on my own. Did she think I'd be old enough soon? I hoped so.

After we got the cinnamon, Juanita wanted to look at some of the other stores. So I took her to my favorite place at the shopping center, the Pet Patch. They had baby guinea pigs for sale.

"I love them!" Juanita clapped.

The baby guinea pigs reminded
me of how small Claude the
Second was when I first brought
him home from the Pet Patch. He
was a lot bigger now, with longer
whiskers.

"Look!" Juanita showed me a
sign. "They're having a super sale.
For thirty dollars you can get a
baby guinea pig and a small cage."

"That's a good price," I said.

"Sí." She nodded. "I have that much. I've been saving."

All the way home, Juanita talked about one baby guinea pig with cinnamon-colored fur.

"Did you see the way she looked at me?" Juanita asked. "So sweet!"

"Have you ever had a pet?" I asked.

"Only goldfish," Juanita said. "There's not much room in a New York City apartment."

"Guinea pigs don't take up much room," I said.

"No, they don't." Juanita smiled.

Just as we reached 29G, Mrs. Ramirez called me over.

"Freddie!" Mrs. Ramirez said. "Our laundry room is still out of order. Can you carry my baskets to Building H?"

Mrs. Tran and Mrs. Ramirez are good friends. If I help one of them, the other one hears about it.

"Go on, Freddie." Juanita stepped inside. "I'll tell your mom where you are."

ZOOM! ZOOM! Zapato!

Mrs. Ramirez had three huge laundry baskets waiting for me. Plus a big bottle of laundry detergent. I'd never run fast with heavy things before. Would my yellow gloves help me do it?

ZOOM! ZOOM! ZaPaTO!

The yellow gloves worked great! In four trips at super speed, I delivered everything to Building H before Mrs. Ramirez had finished walking there.

"You're amazing, Freddie," she said. "Faster than lightning."

Everyone at Starwood Park was used to seeing me disappear with my superpowered purple sneakers. Zapato Power smoke comes out of my heels and makes me invisible when I run.

ZOOM! ZOOM! ZaPaTO!

Uncle Jorge wasn't quite as used to seeing me show up in a cloud of smoke. But he was glad to see me back at 29G.

"Freddie!" he said. "You're just the person I was looking for."

Uncle Jorge was on his way to a gym and wanted to know if I'd like to come too.

He didn't have to ask twice. I hopped into his car.

5. At the Gym

The gym had a wall with free weights of every size lined up. It also had a mirror so you could see yourself being strong.

Uncle Jorge put on some gloves with the fingers cut out. I saw another chance to test my new strength!

"If you're wearing those, can I wear mine?"

I showed him the yellow gloves with the rubber dots on the palms.

"Sure," Uncle Jorge said. "Let's get started."

Uncle Jorge was really strict. He said I couldn't touch anything unless he said it was okay. And first we had to jog in place for a few minutes.

"This is called a warm-up," Uncle Jorge explained. "It gets your muscles ready to exercise."

Uncle Jorge knows a lot about strength training. He said he'd been using weights since my dad taught him how. They used to go to the gym together, before I was born. Uncle Jorge had been a soldier, like my dad. Except Uncle Jorge came home from the war.

"Your dad was a hero, Freddie," Uncle Jorge said. "We will always remember him."

After our warm-up, Uncle Jorge

showed me how to do push-ups.

"I want to see how strong your arms are," he said.

With my yellow gloves, I could do ten push-ups without getting tired.

"*¡Bien hecho!*" Uncle Jorge approved. "Let's try a free weight."

Uncle Jorge gave me a short blue bar with weights on each end. He called it a dumbbell.

"Is it too heavy for your hand?" he asked.

"It's fine," I said.

"Put your arm down by your side and raise the weight by bending your elbow," Uncle Jorge said. "Use a smooth motion."

Uncle Jorge watched my form as I lifted the blue dumbbell eight times with my right hand and eight times with my left.

"Rest," Uncle Jorge said. "Then see if you can lift it for a second set of eight."

I had no trouble lifting the dumbbell again. Uncle Jorge was impressed. We did a few more exercises. I felt so strong with my yellow gloves.

At the end of our workout, we did some stretches to cool down our muscles.

"Now you know the basics," Uncle Jorge said as we left.

In the car on the way home, Uncle Jorge wanted to talk about David.

"Your mom says she's getting really close to her boyfriend," Uncle Jorge said. "Are you okay with that?"

"David makes Mom smile," I told Uncle Jorge. "And he's really nice to me."

"Good to know." Uncle Jorge nodded.

When we got home, Aunt Angela and Puppy were outside near the curb.

RUFF! RUFF!

"This dog needs a walk before we have dinner," Aunt Angela said.

She handed me some plastic bags.

SNIFF! SNIFF!

Puppy sniffed every blade of grass,

looking for the right place to do his business. My guinea pig drops tiny pellets wherever he is. Not Puppy. I wondered why dogs were so particular about where they pooped.

Then I saw something else that puzzled me. Juanita came out of the laundry room for Building G. The door had an OUT

OF ORDER sign on it. What was she doing in there?

RUFF! RUFF!

Puppy spotted Mr. Vaslov and pulled me toward him before I could find out.

RUFF! RUFF!

Mr. Vaslov rubbed Puppy's ears while we talked.

"I really like the yellow gloves you gave me," I said.

Mr. Vaslov looked at my hands. "You're still wearing them."

"They're special," I said.

"If you say so, Freddie." Mr. Vaslov looked puzzled.

I wasn't sure what to say next. Mr. Vaslov liked to test things. He always tested his inventions many times. I needed to prove to him that the yellow gloves gave me extra strength.

"I lifted weights at a gym today," I began. "My uncle said I am strong."

"He's right," Mr. Vaslov answered. "I saw you help me clean up the laundry room and carry heavy baskets for Mrs. Tran."

Why did Mr. Vaslov think that was normal for me? When I ran fast with my superpowered purple sneakers, we both knew it was Zapato Power. But Mr. Vaslov didn't invent my yellow gloves. Mr. Vaslov's meteorite gave them their power. Was it something that would last? Maybe I needed to wait and test my yellow gloves more. A good scientist gathers as many facts as possible.

6. Juanita's Secret

Mr. Vaslov came to my house at six o'clock for Sunday dinner. He's a good friend, and Mom invites him every week. David always eats with us on Sunday too, and he usually helps Mom cook.

Not that Sunday. David came dressed in a suit, straight from his business meeting. Mom told him to stay out of the kitchen and spend time with her big brother.

"Jorge," Mom said with a beaming smile on her face. "This is David. *Mi novio.*"

At first, David and Uncle Jorge were like Juanita and Puppy. David stayed on the other side of the room with Mr. Vaslov, as far away from Uncle Jorge as possible.

Then Uncle Jorge saw David pop a peppermint into his mouth.

"I like those," Uncle Jorge said. "Do you have any extra?"

Sharing candy made a

difference. A few minutes later, they were talking.

"My little sister said you fly drones," Uncle Jorge said. "Tell me about them."

It's never hard to get David to talk about drones. It's his hobby.

"Rosa and Freddie go to the park

with me," David said. "We have
picnics and take turns flying."

"Sounds nice." Uncle Jorge
nodded. "I'd like to go with you
one day."

My uncle winked at me. That's
when I knew he'd decided that
David was all right.

We sat down for dinner and stayed a long time. Everybody was smiling and talking except Juanita.

"Can I please leave the table?" she asked. "I'd like to make a phone call."

As soon as Aunt Angela said it was okay, Juanita had a question for me.

"Can I use your bedroom, Freddie? I'd like some privacy."

I didn't mind letting Juanita use my room, but I thought it was strange. Juanita was going to miss dessert.

"Teenage girls need time alone," Aunt Angela said.

After dinner I went to my bedroom, expecting to see Juanita still on her cell phone. Instead, she was climbing in through my first-floor window!

"Hi, Freddie," she said, lifting her leg over the sill. "I just went out for some air."

Air? Through my bedroom window? Why didn't she use the front door?

Juanita didn't stay to answer. Aunt Angela was calling her.

I felt confused. Should I tell a grown-up that Juanita climbed through my window?

Maybe I should wait till I had more facts to be sure Juanita was doing something wrong. She was my cousin. I wanted us to be friends. To be family.

WHEET! WHEET!

Claude the Second squealed in his cage for a bedtime snack.

I picked up a package of hay, his second-favorite treat next to carrots.

"This is strange too," I said out loud.

The bag was almost empty. It had been full last night. What had happened?

On Monday morning Juanita was still acting funny. She opened the refrigerator and took out a bag of baby carrots, the kind I give to Claude the Second.

"Can I have some of these?" she asked.

"Whatever you want," Mom said, pouring coffee.

Who eats vegetables for breakfast? Something didn't seem right with my new cousin. Juanita put the carrots in her pocket, not in her mouth.

I followed her down the hall to my bedroom. She opened the window again and climbed out.

Where was she going?

I gave Juanita a head start. Then I climbed out too, tiptoeing behind her, down the sidewalk, around the corner, and into the laundry room.

"What are you doing in here?" I asked.

Juanita spun around, her eyes wide. I stood in the doorway, waiting for answers.

"Remember the baby guinea pig we saw at the pet store?" she began.

I nodded. "The one with cinnamon-colored fur."

"She's mine now," Juanita explained. "While you were at the gym, I went back to the store and bought her."

"And you didn't tell your mom?" I asked.

"I will," Juanita promised,

"before we go back to New York."

She led me to a far corner of the laundry room where there was a small cage, the same one we saw on sale at the Pet Patch.

"I named her Cinnamon," Juanita said as we crouched down.

There was nothing to see except an open cage door.

"No!" Juanita cried. "She escaped!"

We searched around the washers and the dryers. Under the sink. On the tall laundry shelves. No Cinnamon.

"What should we do?" Juanita asked.

"She might come out for food," I said.

"I hope so," Juanita cried.

7. The Laundry Room

Juanita took the carrots out of her pocket and set them down. We stepped back and watched through the open laundry room door.

"She's still hiding," Juanita said. "How does she know the food is there?"

"She doesn't have to see it," I

told Juanita. "Guinea pigs have a great sense of smell."

My plan worked. Cinnamon poked her tiny head out from behind the trash can and waddled up to the carrots.

Juanita charged in with her hands out, ready to grab Cinnamon.

WHEET! WHEET! Cinnamon

dashed past me out the door.

Guinea pigs can run really fast for an animal with very short legs. Of course, I can go faster with my superpowered shoes. I circled Building G.

ZOOM! ZOOM! ZAPATO!

I have other powers with my Zapato Power shoes. The smoke that comes out of my heels, making me invisible, also gives me sharper eyesight. And the buttons on my wristband can give me super hearing and super bounce. None of those extra powers helped me find an itty-bitty guinea pig who was scared and hiding.

"She won't come out," I said. "Not when she can smell us."

"We need someone who can smell her," Juanita said.

"Puppy!" we said at the same time.

We were right by 28G, so it took no time at all to put Puppy on his leash.

RUFF! RUFF!

Puppy sniffed the grass like he did before pooping, then he headed toward the bushes, nose pointed to the ground.

RUFF! RUFF!

"He smells something!" Juanita clapped.

Finding Cinnamon wasn't the same as catching her. She scooted out of the bushes and across the grass.

RUFF! RUFF!

I held tightly onto Puppy's leash while Juanita chased after Cinnamon. They ran toward 28G, just as Aunt Angela opened the door.

"What is that?" Aunt Angela screamed.

A little ball of fur ran past her foot into the apartment.

ZOOM! ZOOM! ZAPATO!

In a swirl of smoke, I dropped Puppy's leash and closed the door. BANG! Cinnamon was safely inside 28G.

And Juanita was outside, facing her mother with the truth.

"*Lo siento*," Juanita said. "I should have asked you first."

RUFF! RUFF! Puppy barked and jumped by the door.

"We have to keep that dog away

71

from Cinnamon," Juanita said. "He could hurt her."

"And we need Cinnamon's cage," I added. "It's in the laundry room."

"Go get it, Freddie." Aunt Angela took Puppy's leash.

ZOOM! ZOOM! ZaPaTO!

I raced around Building G to the laundry room and found someone else there. Mr. Willis, the plumber, was beside the tall metal shelves, working on the broken pipe. We knew each other from the times he'd come to help Mr. Vaslov at Starwood Park.

"How's it going?" I asked.

"This pipe is stubborn." He tugged on it.

I took my yellow gloves out of my pocket so I could offer to help. That's when I saw something bad.

Mr. Willis lost his grip on the stubborn pipe and fell backward.

On the way down, he reached for the shelves but ended up pulling them down on himself. BOOM!

I rushed over. "Are you all right?"

Mr. Willis moaned underneath the tall metal shelves.

This was it! The big test for my extra strength. Would my gloves work?

Using both hands I pushed the shelves over and off Mr. Willis.

He turned to the side, touching his head.

"Do you need an ambulance?" I asked.

"No, Freddie. It's okay," he said. "I was just stunned, that's all."

I helped Mr. Willis stand up.

"You're a strong boy, Freddie," he said. "Thank you!"

It sure felt good saving a grown-up.

But someone else needed saving too. Cinnamon!

I picked up her cage and waved goodbye to Mr. Willis.

ZOOM! ZOOM! ZAPATO!

8. Final Test

Puppy was still outside 28G. Except not with the person I expected. Juanita was petting his back.

"*¡Qué perro tan dulce!*" she said.

Juanita had made friends with Puppy. So had Aunt Angela.

"Animals are sweet," she said.

"Maybe it's time we had one in our lives."

"Really?" Juanita asked her mom.

Aunt Angela nodded. "Let's talk after you've rescued the baby guinea pig."

Juanita and I went into 28G with Cinnamon's cage. She was standing in the middle of the living room. YAY!

Except as soon as she saw us, she squealed and ran under the couch.

With my yellow gloves, I pushed the couch forward.

WHEET! WHEET!

Moving the couch didn't help.

Cinnamon ran to another room to hide under a bed.

WHEET! WHEET!

When I crawled under the bed, she dashed behind a dresser.

"This isn't working," Juanita said.

No, it wasn't. We needed brainpower.

"Can we trap Cinnamon?" Juanita asked. "With some kind of basket?"

"A laundry basket!" we shouted together.

I didn't know which closet had a basket in 28G, but I did know where a basket was in my house.

"Wait here!" I told Juanita.

ZOOM! ZOOM! ZAPATO!

In a blink I was back with
Mom's small laundry basket and
guinea pig food.

"Good thinking!" Juanita said.
"Now we have everything we need
to trap Cinnamon."

Guinea pigs do love to eat. This
time, when Cinnamon smelled
food and came out, we plopped the
laundry basket over her.

"We did it!" Juanita cheered.

Together we put Cinnamon into

her cage and walked outside.

RUFF! RUFF!

Aunt Angela was standing there with Puppy.

"Show me our new family pet." She smiled.

Juanita hugged her mom. A nice thing to do. Except it made Aunt Angela drop Puppy's leash.

RUFF! RUFF!

And of course Puppy saw a squirrel.

"Go after him!" Aunt Angela took Cinnamon's cage from my hands.

ZOOM! ZOOM! ZAPATO!

I caught up with Puppy near Building C, where Amy lived. She was home from visiting her grandparents for the weekend.

"Hi, Freddie! What did you do while I was gone?"

"A lot!" I told Amy about the secret guinea pig and all the times Puppy ran off.

While she listened, she looked at my hands.

"Freddie?" she asked. "Where did you find my yellow gloves?"

"In Mr. Vaslov's toolshed," I
answered. "I didn't know they were
yours."

"That's okay," Amy answered. "I
lost them outside."

Amy would be surprised to hear
her gloves got special powers from
the meteorite. How would she
handle extra strength? Would the

gloves work as well for her as they did for me?

There was only one way to find out. A scientific test. Amy had to try the gloves and see.

RUFF! RUFF!

Puppy was pulling on his leash again. I could handle him. Could Amy? Would the gloves help? I pulled them off my hands and gave them back to her. Once she had them on, I asked for a favor.

"Would you mind holding Puppy's leash?"

RUFF! RUFF!

A squirrel whizzed by. Amy held

on with both hands, doing her best as Puppy yanked her along. Since she's a first grader, she's lots smaller than me.

"Whoa!" Amy cried. "This dog is strong!"

The yellow gloves didn't help Amy hold onto Puppy. He pulled away.

RUFF! RUFF!

Hmm. What did this mean? Was I strong, just like Mr. Willis said? Did I move the metal shelves and the couch all on my own? Could I lift weights and carry heavy baskets by myself?

What an awesome thought!

"Why are you smiling, Freddie?" Amy asked. "Puppy just ran off."

"No problem," I said, touching the button on my wristband. "I have super speed."

I also have super bounce. Since I was in such a good mood, I pressed an extra button to make my shoes bounce me into the air as I followed Puppy

back to 28G.

Boing! Boing! Boing!

RUFF! RUFF!

I picked up Puppy's leash as Aunt Angela came out with a doggy treat. He lunged for it. Hard. I held on tightly. No yellow gloves needed.

Uncle Jorge came out with his car keys.

"Freddie!" he said. "Do you want to go back to the gym today?"

Absolutely! I couldn't wait to see what else I could do with my bare hands.

Don't Miss Freddie's Other Adventures!

PB 978-0-8075-9479-7

PB 978-0-8075-9483-4

PB 978-0-8075-9484-1

HC 978-0-8075-9485-8
PB 978-0-8075-9486-5

PB 978-0-8075-9496-4

HC 978-0-8075-9497-1
PB 978-0-8075-9499-5

HC 978-0-8075-9500-8
PB 978-0-8075-9542-8

HC 978-0-8075-9539-
PB 978-0-8075-9559-

HC 978-0-8075-9544-2
PB 978-0-8075-9563-3

HC 978-0-8075-9562-6
PB 978-0-8075-9567-1

HC 978-0-8075-9570-1
PB 978-0-8075-9572-5